falling hard

falling hard

100 love poems by teenagers

edited by
BETSY FRANCO

CANDLEWICK PRESS
CAMBRIDGE, MASSACHUSETTS

First edition 2008

Library of Congress Cataloging-in-Publication Data

Falling hard : 100 love poems by teenagers / edited by Betsy Franco. — 1st ed.
p. cm.
ISBN 978-0-7636-3437-7
[1. Children's poetry — American. 2. Love — Juvenile poetry. 3. Youth's writings — American.]
I. Franco, Betsy. II. Title.
PS586.3F35 2008
811'.608 — dc22   2007022401

2 4 6 8 10 9 7 5 3 1

Printed in the United States of America

This book was typeset in Garamond Ludlow Light.

Candlewick Press
2067 Massachusetts Avenue
Cambridge, Massachusetts 02140

visit us at www.candlewick.com

For D. F.

Contents

Introduction

Falling Hard is a rousing, uncensored discussion of love by contemporary teenagers from all over the world. It moves from innocent love to unrequited love, from love endings to self-respect, from self-love to love with a touch of realism.

The poetry is honest, edgy, fearless, emotional, and wise. Even the most despondent poems have energy, which ultimately translates to hope.

Love is well observed, as in "Our eternal happiness now eternally gone." Poets are direct: "Let me break it down for you like an inverse haiku: / *I will not have sex with you.*" And their inventiveness is refreshing, as exemplified by "Making Love to Shakespeare." Throughout the collection, teenage writers pull the covers on themselves, whether it be "kissing strange boys behind the haunted subway" or admitting "I freak out about love . . . I'm in disguise when I love."

This collection was mainly compiled via e-mail. Initially, I didn't know if some of the writers were male or female; if they were from Harlem or Kirkwood, Missouri; if the e-mail was coming from two blocks away in Palo Alto, California, or continents away in Australia. I was fortunate to receive submissions from a diverse group of poets. As far as I know, from within the United States, they were African-American, Asian-American, Latino/a, American Indian, and Iranian-American, and from outside the country, they were British, Australian, Macedonian, and Canadian. They were straight, gay, lesbian, transgender, and bi. They were autistic. They were aspiring writers, and they were teenagers who had written only one poem, ever.

I could have composed a poem from the creative e-mail addresses of all the poets. Instead, I'm presenting their poems, sharply personal and profoundly universal.

Think about it. Who better to discuss the nuances of love's joy and pain than teenagers? ✳

✳✳✳✳✳

Sitting on the porch swing
amidst the sea of suburbia
where cookie-cutter souls
come home every day at 5 to the raised ranch

she strolls on by in her arcane soignée style
playing her saxophone to a haunting melody
so the whole wide world can hear her
her motives, an enigma
yet she charms us all with her sophistication
her difference in this world

how I long to meet her
get whisked away by her song
yet mother says I'm still too infatuated
to cross the street
and far too young for jazz

JOSEPH LINDBLAD, age 14

✳✳✳✳✳

Tilt the halo over my head
I don't care what the caution tape read
It's time to get a little dangerous
Let's fall in love.

Forget the scriptures, forget the past
Conscience and common sense never last
It's time to get a little curious
Let's fall in love.

RACHEL McCARREN, age 15

At work

There's actually only one thing I care about.
It's a girl with brown hair and brown eyes
She's short, she comes up to my shoulders or my chin
Today I was going to ask her a question,
has anyone ever fallen in love with you while you work?
Because, I wanted to tell her, I always fall in love
with girls like you.
She called my name from the other room
I was washing dishes
She asked me if the music was alright,
it was Simon and Garfunkel—here's to you Mrs. Robinson.
When she came in, soapy handed I mentioned
that I needed to see The Graduate again
She'd never seen it she said. Who's in that?
Dustin Hoffman.

NICK ROSS-RHUDY, age 17

Gift

I would break you make you
breathe hard for me,
take in more air,
as if I was there to breathe it too.
        Nonsense
nonsuchaswe
could survive this journey.
I would score you bleed you
scream you,
find you unwanting, unlacking,
in everything I want.
You are a thesaurus with no
                words, book of my heart
        and sickened stomach.
I would ask you where you stand,
        if I did not know you better
                I would say you float:
Delicate.
                Your name spells ornate strength.
You are the castle I point for,
        gaining power as I go up the clouds,
out of breath:
Keep breathing for me
        breathe harder,
take in more air,
as if I was there
to breathe it too.

Lost maps and a few countries later
I could drive under your window,
Couldn't I?
And ask how have you been have you got enough time
to go for a drive?

But what I'll really mean is
are you ready to dive in?
This is not falling,
        this is landing.

PORTIA CARRYER, age 16

Reminisce

The memory of the touch of a friend
(or is he so much more?)
brings forth such painful happiness,
as lines of heat, scorched by skin,
rush along the path his arms once took.

Holding himself against me
(or is it me against him?),
arms draped over my shoulders,
and joined at my solar plexus,
a light touch in a heavy time.

Time passes slowly by,
and his arms move with the clock;
arms around my chest,
clasping above my navel,
hearts race and smiles cost nothing.

He lies across my lap
and I hold him close.
We drift near to sleep, his head
resting gently on my palm
and mine on his shoulder blade.

Eyes slip shut and I struggle,
barely winning the fight
against the time-thief, sleep.
The clock (the killer) beckons us.
It is time to leave and parting hurts for both.

ROSS LEACH, age 14

Punch-drunk Love

With you I'm always speeding,
zig-zagging 'cross double yellow lines,
eyes closed in ecstasy.
When the familiar siren's scream approaches—
"Pull over on the right shoulder at the next exit"—
I'll blame you.
When my eyes can't follow the jerking
motion of his finger across my sight—
"Don't move your head ma'am,
just your eyes"—
and when he clucks his tongue in disapproval—
"I'm gonna have to ask you
to step out of the car"—
and when he takes out the Breathalyzer—
"Now stand straight,
feet together,
arms at your sides"—
my blood-alcohol level will be off the charts
with lust.

I still can't imagine
Why he won't believe me
When I tell him
All I've had to drink tonight
Is you.

ELLIE MOORE, age 16

I Love You

Looking into your eyes, my heart skips a beat,
and it makes me want to vomit.
You mean the world to me,
and I hate that.
I love you with all my heart,
so I think I'll kill myself.
You make me feel like no one else can,
so I know I can't trust you.
You are my one, my only
piece of shit that I can't stand.
I love you.

ALANA GRACIA SOPKO, age 14

Addiction

I love Black Women . . .
tall, short, skinny, even medium.
I love to be w/ you Black Woman.

Queen of Big Breasts, Just Right Breasts,
Full Lips, Wide Hips,
even your Backyard makes me want to take full trips.

I love you, Black Woman, darker than
night itself, sweeter than
molasses on a sugarcane.

I love you, Black Woman . . .
skin complexion of many colors:
caramel, chocolate, butter pecan,
honey, toffee, root beer, even French vanilla.

(But these qualities and complexions
only satisfy $\frac{1}{4}$ of me.)

Black Woman, you have the mind of a poet, writer,
doctor, computer engineer, physicist,
model, and entertainer.
I love you for your mind the most.

If it wasn't for you, Black Woman, I wouldn't
be here right now.
I wouldn't be the tall, handsome, strong,
Never-Ignorant-Getting-Goals-Accomplished
Man I am today.

Black Woman . . .

Damn,

Black Women.

DAMON KEITH KIMBROUGH (KARMA), age 17

Lorraine V

You know, I saw you
slipping your skin into the fountain.
I wanted to hide, cover
my eyes with the back of my hand
but I had to look
had to watch you step into pale water
and give away the warmth I wanted to hoard
like chestnuts,
or diamonds,
or zippers that you wore.

LUKE M. RICKFORD, age 17

My Love Line Color Spectrum

I talk to boys as if they were colors
Like when I'm on the phone with *Eric
I'm in green mode, just thinking about all
the gifts he's going to give me when he
comes over! Talk about $ signs.
But when I'm on the phone with *Chris,
I'm in yellow mode just wondering if he's
playing mind games with me, by telling me
what I want to hear!
*Rob is so blue. He tells me all his problems
and how he's so sorry for telling me about his day
and not worrying about mine!
Oh, but when I'm on the phone with *Mike, I'm in
red mode, just thinking about how he's cheating on me
with my best friend's neighbor.
And *Derrick, he has me in orange mode.
He's so sweet to me and obeys me as if I am his queen.
Then there's *Phil. That's when I'm in white mode because
our relationship is so blank. He's next on my hit list!
And last but not least, there's *Sam. He's my
favorite out of the love line. When I'm with him,
I'm the whole color spectrum!

LARELLE KING, age 15

Making Love to Shakespeare

I thought about you today,
could almost remember your lips,
firm and smooth,
and your tongue, juicy as grapefruit.
Your eyes were two black fires burning in grass-rimmed wells
(I wondered how many others had seen their fish-eyed faces
reflected in those irises).

I remember how I laughed
when your unkempt goatee tickled my stomach,
how all those ruffles on your shirt got in the way,
the heat, the solidity of your heaving chest.

I remember how you held my chin,
carefully in your hand,
at arm's length,
so you could reflect on my visage
with Hamlet's discerning eye,
though whenever you were with me,
it was never a question of
"To be or not to be."

I do remember your mouth,
how it curled up on the right in Puck-like pleasure
because you knew exactly what I was thinking
(I never was a very good actress).
And I remember that smirk,
not unlike Iago's twisted resolve,
as you split my corset in twain.

I would have painted an inch thick
and laughed honest and constant as rain
if you had called me your Muse.

I vaguely remember your bed like a furnace,
how your sweat tasted salty as mine,
your hot, whispering eloquence in my ear,
and your hands calloused and ink-stained.

I shall never forget
your parenthetical frame
hunched over a bleeding manuscript.
While you scribbled furiously,
brow furrowed,
inwardly cursing whoever invented
such a slow-moving quill,
I lay curled in your sheets,
wishing my blood were your ink,
my body your pen,
staining those immortal words,
etching eternal eloquence.
O! If only it could have been
my name you muttered feverishly
instead of the Lady Macbeth.

I thought about you today.
But when I flipped to the back of the book, and saw
your name scrawled 'neath that ridiculous picture,
I scoffed

at your dog collar,
those muttonchop sideburns
encroaching on such an unsightly face,
a beard pointed as Satan's.
That wasn't the Billy I remembered
from my seventeen-year-old daydreams.

I refuse to believe you've grown cold and blue,
that such a body could ever turn to dust.
I could just tell from the way you wrote,
you had to be beautiful.

ELLIE MOORE, age 16

New Friend in Mexico

I met my sober friend
I met my love kid
When she watches scenery I bet she feels the same as me
I met my butterfly
I met my bed buddy
And when she listens to a song I know she feels it all night long
She's my motorcycle
She's my cigarette
When the night's this quiet I think I can hear her thinking
She's a firecracker
She's a pretty girl
She's a shadow on the wall
I'm a shadow on the wall.

NICK ROSS-RHUDY, age 17

Regardless

The phone rings
I feel a rush
the doorbell rang
it was you

I love you

the cops came
they asked me questions
they were looking for you

I love you

the boys came
they swore and broke the windows
it was your fault

I love you

she asked where her money was
I knew it was you

I love you

we robbed the woman
I handed you $500
you disappeared
you're a thief

I love you

you did that crazy thing to me and her
it felt good
it was you

I love you

as we rode side by side
metal locking our wrists
we smiled

I love you

LISA VUOLO, age 15

Untitled

Every time he gets around me
I fall weak
Trip on my words
Suddenly can't speak

The way he licks his lips
Soft and wet
My palms get sweaty
My heart jets

He inspires me
To be everything I can
It's crazy how I feel this way
About another man

He calls my name
Like the lyrics to a love song
Carried to me by Cupid
Nothing can go wrong

When I look at him, same body as me
I get scared and back away
Somehow, he makes me smile again
and the feelings I have convince me to stay

ALJUNE, age 17

＊＊＊＊＊

We were always looking for the highest place,
where the sun would soar the longest
and nest in the branches of the tallest trees.
Laughing, we raced across the field.
You turned to wait for me, your breath already calm,
your hands steadying me, touching my hair.
I remember falling, pressed together
like the blackberries we crushed in our mouths—
above us only sky
and in your eyes, when they were open,
that same clear blue.

MARI, age 16

Love Poem

I am
the flour
to your tortilla,
baby.

JUAN NUNEZ, age 15

Pledge of Affection to a Nerd

I . . .

. . . drift, lazy, on the comforting breeze
as you rhythmically speak:
computer jargon.

. . . can't get over how blue your eyes are:
talking about *Star Wars.*

. . . couldn't be prouder of you as you recite:
forty-seven digits of pi.

. . . will listen, though I may never understand:
you beat the final level of Escape from Mordor!

. . . want to stay in your arms all evening while you talk about:
ancient war strategy, lunar eclipses, molecules . . .

whispering sweet algorithms in my ear.

LAURA TABOR, age 16

✳✳✳✳✳

I flex my muscles,
sitting in a lawn chair.
Red and violet dance exuberantly across the sky.
Waves crash gracefully along the shore.
Seagulls caw in the distance.
Before my heavy eyelids fall,
I stare at the empty lawn chair beside me
and I think   about what it would be like
        if that lawn chair were filled.

MICHAEL STERN, age 12

fingerstrings

bristle clean tidy blond strands
and here come I to ruin them with
fingertips piercing light gold traveling
down
  down
    down
till I reach the end
      and start back up at the top
we're silent
contending with our own thoughts
thinking about touches
              and tickles
              and time
                        and distance.
this is not my home.

but if it were,
      this is where I'd be

all the time.

HARRIS LAPIROFF, age 16

Kitchen Stranger

Tell me
how it all happens when
I find you on the steps and
you offer to carry a grocery
bag to the kitchen and hold the
little stool while I put the
cans on the topmost shelf

And you come with
daisies hidden in your jacket
pocket so there are petals falling
and smelling of your cigarettes and
you, an excuse, tried to mumble but
all I remembered was the clumsy
way your shirt collar was tucked

And tell me
how I answer someone when
all I know myself is that I
liked it when I caught
you watching me in the stainless-
steel reflection of the fridge though
I should've told you to stop because
staring men leave nothing behind but
coffee stains on my countertop

Instead I kept quiet and talked
of the weather, though we both
knew it was never about
the temperature nor the time of
the sunset

JOHAINA CRISOSTOMO, age 16

Love Song

I see her and I hear a song
I kiss her and silently sing along

Her melody caught me stone cold
Harmony makes her whole and when she comes
I don't want her to go

I just want to keep her coming
just want to keep her strumming me in her arms,
playing her guitar

Dear love,
Oh love,
How I wonder what you are

It's funny how reality seems so far from this dream come true
I'm not trying to write no love poem
I just gotta tell you 'bout this love song that I heard
on the third of November

I can't remember ever feeling this way
wanting to say what I'm at a loss for words for
I just want to hear more of what tastes like
the best sense of musical evidence
hidden under silence and
"I know something you don't know's"

like we
take off our clothes
and mold
until
she loses her hold
so
give me a smile world
because
music has got a love Jones

DENESHEA RICHEY, age 15

The Pond Is Dry Now

I remember
when we were younger
we kept a toad together as a pet,
and called him Frog.
We danced on grass in Summer
and lay warm together during Winter. And Frog was happy
to ribbit between us, his great mouth billowing
while we laughed just to hear each other.

When you moved away,
I let you keep Frog, but he must have been sad.
He died soon after. You told me over the phone,
but you didn't cry.

I guess you had him dried or stuffed or else
squashed, and now he's locked in some big chest,
lonely in your attic.

Where I suppose you are too.

J MIDGLEY, age 16

The secret lives of sea turtles

She looked at him with the tiny
    Puffy eyes
        Of a virgin
            Flesh illuminated
                All crashing under a canopy of ceiling
            And the immense night
        She tried typing her name with her tongue
    Along his mouth,
His ear and the slender side of his shoulder

They rolled across the bed,
    Back and forth like waves in sultry brine
        Breaking in the taste of skin,
            The soft arch and curve
        Of the calf
    She yielded

A slated moon,
   Eyes the size of waxy marbles
      And a provoked song
         That twists around the savvy mallows of her hips
      The slight of her skinny elbows
   And the tender, solid space of her armpits.

HANNAH SHR, age 15

✳✳✳✳✳

(a small warm dimly lit living room with a woven mexican rug on the floor. a boy sits hunched cross-legged on the floor, wearing gray slacks, a black dress shirt untucked, and slippers. an empty wine bottle and an empty wine glass sit next to him.)

BOY

plus i don't normally drink.

look, if my eyes were cameras i could show you what i mean.

on the other hand, if life were a film would it really be as perfect as i keep promising?

on the other hand, i don't want to be cliché. my favorite word these days.

trying to make things sound good you forget what you're trying to say.

what do i want.

a girl in a summer dress.

at the river.

a slice of watermelon at watermelon beach.

a glass of water. could i have a glass of water with my pancakes?

could i have some rainbows on the wooden walls?

could i have some prehistoric fish/submarines chilling where the paint cracked?

could i have some conversations with spiders?

i want conversations with spiders.

i really want that. i'm not just saying that to stay on top of the game.

i want that.

i really want to scream with my window rolled down.
in mexico i wasn't as cool, but maybe life was more real.
memories really stick to me now.
but they make me lonely.

the best feelings, you never can put your finger on them.
on the other hand, there are things like kissing.
i don't fuckin care how things turn out.
i'm not saying i'm going to make stupid decisions.
but what really matters is the moment.
those kisses and nothing else.

(slowly fade to black.)

NICK ROSS-RHUDY, age 17

He does.

He always satisfies me.

Breaking zealously the chords of a hyped lust for skin sliding off, he jars my center to life, writing me the pages to a successful climb. Granted, he never instigates. He awaits my sine-flavored longing and subdues me into his accompaniment. He lies, patiently receiving and docile to the touch. I can play my 5-legged spiders over his entirety, bottle the moans I lure from his depths, to let every pair feel our night. Pulling him taut and testing his throbbing reaction, I know he is ready for my every move.

No sir, my piano never fails me.

MARGARET H. SAMUELS, age 16

That Fucking Zip and Zap

Unquestionable intelligence is certainly
A most rare trait in this bleak
Seascape, the mass of grey humanity,
And certainly why I love that man.

Mental stimulation
is (and back and forth)
equal (and zip and zap)
To the carnal joy of the flesh.
Body screams with adolescent glee
And is shot, killed by that bond
Which only in equal minds of equal people
Is present.

We understand each other,
Although I don't understand why.
Who'da thought that such great friendship
(or whatever one may call it)
Could, by chance, be found.

It's just that fucking zip and zap.

ROSS LEACH, age 14

Mine of miles

I believe your voice,
when I hear it.
I miss you, you say.
There is a well in those words,
dark and slippery even in
the face of day.
Every line I speak
is an echo of Shakespeare:
Shall I compare thee to a summer's day?

You fall, in autumn,
New England style.
I would like to see
those miles you've traveled and told me of:
the deep south in summer
inside Massachusetts
the dust of Central America.
I would like
to see you, again.

Anne Sexton, seeped in madness and beauty
Sylvia Plath, one of the most beautiful women
Adrienne Rich, who did not commit suicide
Shakespeare, who brings me nervous to your side

I would like
to spend the coin of my days
at your ear.
I keep fear at my shoulder,

not wanting to
overextend
your patience.

Sonnet LXXX
The worst was this; my love was my decay.
Sonnet LXI
For thee watch I whilst thou dost wake elsewhere,
From me far off, with others all too near.
My legs crossed on the grass,
I turn the thin pages of *The Complete Poems* of Anne Sexton.
At home, I let *The Early Years* of Adrienne Rich fall open
to a random page.

I don't know
what your voice belies.
I speak softly,
not wanting to give too much away.
I don't want to be the one
to cry.

I miss you, too, I reply.

PORTIA CARRYER, age 16

How I Fell in Love

His eyes are endless in a deep pool of beauty
And I want to put on my swimsuit and swim around
in them.
His voice is as soft as a baby's whisper.
I love every waking moment with him. I also love
the non-waking moments.
He is my first, my last, my everything, and my second,
my third, my fourth.
He comes from the eastside where there is a church and
liquor store on almost every corner. Where I started from.
He'll give me the stars, the moon, and the sun.
How about the Milky Way, and the planets, too?
I wonder how he got me to fall in love with him.

JENNIFER HOLMAN, age 17

Look at my feet

Your hair is a chicken salad
Your forehead, an apple, extra fancy
Your nose, a flat steak
Your ears, paper plates of a stegosaurus
While you examine my attractive feet,
Let me assure you
That it would be acceptable for you to eat my leg
I want to sneak you into my ginger ale
You are a rhinoceros . . .
And I would not hesitate to follow you for days in
the savannah.

SEPH KRAMER, age 16

Who I Am and What I Need

I am not despondent, but hopeful.
I am not happy, but oh well. I am
Being penetrated by these thoughts
Of lust
Love
Fag
Rise above
The rest of them
Kiss a guy, get a man
Be a bi, lend a hand
Join a club, be proud
Get (a guy) to shout out loud
That he loves me!

I'll fucking tell you that
I need a guy
Maybe I'm not bi
Cuz all I have now is lust
For someone lacking a bust
I don't care about Rachel
Don't care about Leigh
All I want is a man to love and cherish me
Going crazy
Dazed and hazy
Soon I'm going to go to school
Is being gay cool?

ANONYMOUS, age 14

Jump. Don't Trip.

Let's jump to conclusions
Lay out all the expectations
Doubt each other from the start
Put up all our walls
Never open up
Let's try to forget we're falling hard
Keep all our thoughts tied up
All our words at the backs of our throats
Bite our tongues
Swallow the inevitable
Live for the days spent alone
Just us.
Pretend to be something we're not
If only for a day
If only for a week
If only for a year
Let's take this one second at a time
Tread carefully
You don't stand a chance
If you're going to take the fall
Jump.
Don't trip.
Make it count.
Do it with poise.

JESSICA C. GALENTE, age 17

Hungry

I know what you meant when you said
words sound differently out loud,
and I cover my face
because
I'm afraid of what I say.
I can hear you're hungry
when I lay my head on your belly.
So desperate to hear such a sound again,
I starve myself into oblivion
tonight.

SANDRA GEORGIJEVSKA, age 17

Of Infatuation and Nicotine Fits

Tonight
she'll relight dead cigarettes for strangers,
staining filters with battery-acid lipstick imprints,
giving masturbatory glances as she hands them back.
Synapses will crackle as we swallow foreign objects,
and justify genesis with wasted minds.

> "Eyes like opium dens," they whisper in the smoke,
> clutching velveteen existence with white-knuckled fists.
> Inhaling the hormonal discharge of her offerings
> as they dance with obese mannequins.

Oh, tonight.

Tonight she will wear a cardigan the color of bile,
and we'll move through the swarm at a glacial crawl;
watching her Pulp haircut sway in static air
as I contemplate yesterdays spent
examining her echo
at The Treblinka.

TIMOTHY G. LARKIN, age 18

Witch's Carol

My demon was a gentle soul.
I touched his cheek as I danced with him,
Caressed the razor-sharp protruding bones, the rapier, and
the wrist guard of iron —
Steel was not yet known to the underworld.
(Alas?)
My partner's fellows mocked him,
Especially for his clumsiness.
He had none of that alluring, wolflike,
Dangerous-and-fiery-yet-perfectly-staged
Grace that the villains always have.
No, he had none of this, and yet
While I held his hand —
Rather, I should say "gnarled claw" —
I felt something unusual between our two hands . . .

But maybe it was just the infusion of mandrake and nightshade,
Which I had applied earlier to my palms to prevent chapping
(a trivial spell, not worth mentioning)
And which was, truth be told, becoming unpleasantly sticky,
Quite gluey and uncomfortable
(for it is hot in hell).

JUSTINE KOO DRENNAN, age 16

Love in the Moonlight

No one knows I'm here.
Silvery strands of moonlight.
Shh. Meet me by the ancient oak.
What bird will dare but the great horned owl?
The fire within my heart burns only for you.
Do you love me too?

DILLON YORK, age 13

Like Sex, an Orange Is Best Enjoyed Slowly

Lying in the grass, you beautiful goddess
You smell so sweet,
Smooth skin at my fingertips
Glowing radiant orange, the sun in miniature
I can only gaze into those orangey eyes for so long . . .
My tension mounts . . .

I want to consume you, you orangey whore
Watch the sweat drip out of every pore
I want to wrap around you
I want to get inside you
Want to sample the naked flesh within

Ripping off your clothes like they're on fire
Stop, drop, and roll
My horny hands exploring every curve
Tongue ready for citrusy bliss

You thick-skinned primeval woman,
Reveal to me your hidden shame
I savor the forbidden tastes of
Your sweet orangey juices

Our lovemaking
so raw
so innocent
so primal
so right

I cherish our affair
This fundamental consummation of races

I savor our multi-racial relationship
breath exhaled in a smooth hiss,
as I rip you apart
section by section

As my feast concludes
There's nothing left of your old self
You have joined me
Become a part of me

Two halves.
Now one.
Together.
Forever.

RYAN PRIOR, age 16

Jellybones

1.
if you memorized the lines across my palms
the intersections of valleys and scars
the metal bars on the 22 Fillmore
the foil wrapped around burritos
the sweat he blew into me
all folded itself into creases
and curves on my hands
if you memorized these moments of
teenage street sheet naked wispy and dirty
the jagged o's and blazed words of love through
smoke and deadbolts
his fist a seed in my stomach surrounded
by mucus and acid
he was something foreign I held onto like
old pieces of plastic the wind can't claim
if you knew how he was in my walk
his breath on earlobes
persuasive voice a deep ebb
a constant bassline to my
less than consistent little-girl rasp of knuckles and nails
if you knew how his shoulder blades scooped
into V's under my small hands
waiting for warmth and memory
you still wouldn't know
his voice against tin on ocean wire-thin heart
thinner veins
I don't know if you would have felt that thing
creep under feet

unprepared, undisguised
like sidewalk initials
etched into brain folds
smooth and giving like my palms

2.
he told himself
not to sever his hearing and heart
like separating capillaries from a web of tangled regrets
he told himself not to cut deep
and I watch as her heart folds into itself
a square one-inch thick
trying to erase muscle memory like the spray sliding over sand
she curls silently
and I watch ungiving

3.
ivory body
her stomach smoother than sea glass
rippled with his touch
a tide he controlled
since when do brown men's hands
control Moon?
a celestial pull from the ocean shore
split them
open and bleeding

4.

and even writing about it
makes it so much more permanent
she wants her short nails to scar his inner arm
he deserves to hurt
like salt and black smoke under eyelids and nostrils
this is not over
and she cannot let go
it claws at her like love was only an afterthought
to dirty bedsheets and greasy pizza
a girl hurting herself because his cuts don't seem deep
enough already
and teenage love is supposed to be forgotten
with homework and family meals
writing needs to be impermanent for her
susceptible to tearstains, tsunamis
she does not want this to be a witness
a plea
anything of importance
she must convince herself that all this
was less than important

DALIA RUBIANO YEDIDIA, age 16

Deceleration

Some times go by
I wish I weren't alone
The constant wallflower
That gets in the way
'Cause we're all jealous
And maybe if I annoy you enough
You'll break up.

Your hands are screaming across the room
"Let us hold each other!"
The scene so Hollywood it makes me sick.

I will be the fifth wheel
On your automobile
The brakes on a bicycle built for two
Oh, I'll get in the way
So you're never alone.

KATIE CHOW, age 14

Clouded Vision

The skies were cloudy behind her eyes,
Her life darkened without any light,
Still she was alive with laughter,
It was love at first sight for me,
Though she was blind.
I would try to brighten her day,
Fragrant roses anonymously delivered,
Let her know that she was loved
But she still stayed oblivious,
Of her silent suitor.
I finally got up the courage to talk to her,
She seemed amused but not delighted,
She was unaware of her beauty,
So she seemed to think
I was teasing her.
When I made my intentions clear,
Her mood brightened
Because she had never had a boyfriend,
But though she laughed easily,
She had never seen her own smile.
So when I spoke my words of love,
She seemed taken aback,

For her heart, stayed by fear of rejection,
Refused to be given over
To one such as me.
I wanted her then and there,
She was looking too far ahead.
Perhaps she saw some obstacle,
That would make the seeing man stumble.

DANIEL LEICHTLING, age 17

Blackberries

Blackberries smell like my first crush
and laundry
and the first grade playground — only the shady parts —
and my first shot of vodka . . .
Perhaps it's appropriate that they stain.

I am here and no one else's woman
I'm hungrier than a moan
Passion? that's all the fucking recognition I need.

[I would have to love someone who could beat me in a fight]

My insides leak inky black out of my irises
I always bleed
to keep me real and new and godly
Icarus? these wings will never burn.

I want to sin in the hottest loins of the fire
nestle into its downy flames
coal couch so soft in its heat.
I would lie on my bed of sizzling pillows
and dream of rain in the trees.

This is how I long to live
I can see forever through the dip in the mountain's thighs
but the skyline is fraying.

It's a slow compacting of the invisible void around me
all his weight against my plastic bubble
seeing him peering in at me behind my eyelids
reveling in the surface tension
like a burp that tastes of brownies and vomit.

[the nicest thing a boy ever did for me was pull his fingers
out from my sticky insides and taste it
to make sure it wasn't blood]

I can see the look in his mouth
it's sly its hungry puckered
just blank with fuck lust.

Smooth grape-like nudity
his tongue like an ice cube tasting my sweet heat.
He smelt like cinnamon tonight
but soon turned sour in my arms
blinding flashing lightning in my guts
the sun races by like electric worms in hyper-speed
I'm scared I won't be full forever.
A sloppy oops.

Turn my face just the other way
no one would have known
except all the people I told.

Three fingerprints where he touched me with albino hands
Three marks against a tan.

Easy for you to say — you have self-control
another sloppy drunk
another grabby hands
another smirking fuck.
Fuck love — I still carry his poem.

He smokes Marlboro Reds.
He whispers "Oh my god" as I lick his lime lips
and tell myself
to memorize his scent.
musty
sweat
sticky
I had to brush my taste to keep the teeth of him
out of my head.
He tells me I have a cheeky smile.
I grit my teeth and think to myself
"so this is how it's lost"
and
"when will he be done?"

He molds me
I am wax melting away
Suddenly I realize that he doesn't know that I write poetry
and I am seventeen!

22 but just a boy
poisoned lungs
blotted past
there is no pain
just a deaf ramming
I wish he'd be quieter
"You're gorgeous"
"I could make love to you"
breath like wind

I don't care what they tell you girls —
sex is sex
and you can't make love.

*   *   *   *

then calm
a hot shower
steamed mirrors
those hands suddenly so soft
an embrace like crutches keeps me up
so limp
a fleshy shell of exhaustion

*   *   *   *

all I can recall is a distinct sense of dissipation
like mummies turning to sand

leaving only a few Crest-smile sparkles in the air
like lost bubbles

*   *   *   *

flying on wings of hemp and silver
waxing sunlight crackles through dust
gold glass on a poisoned oak
this is how I long to live
naked on the ridge
where no one can see

*   *   *   *

I'm sorry I have nothing to give but I'm
in the process of turning to steel
don't touch me
or you'll burn
or melt
or die . . .

*   *   *   *

nothing but a small black fruit
so bitter on my tongue
blackberries bleed too

EMMA MARLOWE, age 17

✳✳✳✳✳

Love only works in the winter
When it's cold
And you have nothing real to cling to
When you become blind because the world is ugly
And numb
Just as lovers are.

Love has no use here in summerland
Raging out of control
Engulfing
Just like the winter.

SEAN R. BLUM, age 16

A Broken Snow Globe

There's never been an excuse for ignorance.

Just flags and fags and burning bridges,
just lots of ancient skulls. I sat in my room,
aching as deeply as the warrior
whose heart had been pierced by an enemy's spear
in his father's hand.

I liked thinking that every one of the tears,
on its saltwater sojourn down my face,
contained a little universe born of rage.

Wishful thinking; just protein.

I remember wondering at how strange it was that
my father who's always assured me
that the world would turn its back on me
sooner than he,
would rather me be a murderer than a lover of my own gender.

And it wouldn't be so bad, if he didn't claim to love me
"no matter what." I cried for him, and I will
again. The worst thing is my father's love is a burden; he's
become a cold crutch to me, a necessary evil,
something to be waited out; but
my father isn't a storm.

He's the angry tide against my weakening sands,
the frustration that threatens riot over reason,
and I'm worried. I'm worried for him,
and that his last words may be a curse.

I pace, and think of the knives in his heart
from my first true kiss . . .

whenever it may be.

MEHRON ABDOLLMOHAMMADI, age 15

Bodies Can Move This Way (After Lee Ann Brown)

I sleep on the floor.
You wrap your arms around my ass
With the accuracy of choreography
But less intimate than last week.
Bodies can move this way.
In and out of jeans like porn stars.
Only a wall away from a mother
So we whisper to each other's chests,
Kiss in the shape of words.
I forget that your hair is something special,
Tiger stripes on your skin,
Soft as Velcro.
Bodies can move this way,
Fast and practiced.
We lie together on the floor of your room,
My eyelids recede,
Then close.
Yours shut in return.
But mine sneak open to
Watch you.
Bodies can move this way,
But not ours, not anymore,
Because I'm bored.
It's been months since
We've discovered something new.
You invite me off the floor
But I know the squeak of your bed

GIA HARRIS, age 15

Who Are You?

You're not the girl I fell in love with.
Instead you're a monster of brooding beauty,
Your feelings for me a mind myth,
Our love a product of human ingenuity.

SIMON JOHN WILLIAMS, age 16

Psychic Leech

Living with a leech
Burrowed deep within my skin
Teeth piercing flesh
Stealing what's within

Festering, draining, sucking
I disappear more with every step
Consuming, controlling, infecting
My life gets shorter with every breath

This slimy little leech
Loves to sing and dance
It loves to feast
Off of our sweet romance

But I can't peel it off
Without breaking the skin
I can't open the wound
Without letting something else in

So I'll let it stand
Let it suck away what it can
Let it feed off what it steals
Let it never let me heal

This leech is uncontrollable
and I cater to its feast
I'm holding the plate
that feeds the beast

I offer to you, leech
all my flesh and blood
but when you reach my empty core
then slide back in the mud

DUSHAN PERERA, age 16

raspy voices

my head is submerged beneath the warm soothing water
it tickles the hairs on my neck
the same feeling your fingers trace
when you're watching me sleep
the candlelight is oblivious of its ambience
modestly scattered around the echo of the room

i can see the round of my bosoms
the hills of my belly
one side covered by a dark shadow
a red-orange sunset
slinking down the other

the judgment of my plump
is beauty
in your eyes, i am full
i am filled
i am someone

i close my eyes to push down my heart in my throat
and the weight of the water on my chest
is a painful reminder of your head
laying atop my soft pillow breasts
and i'm pleading for your remainder
your security
your certainty

i want to come home to the smell of your cologne
know the colors of your clothes
touch the smooth of your back
and contrast your strength
with your gentle being
arms around me
this is our spoon
our usual, our ritual of affection

our eyes are closed
you utter "how are you" and wait
for my belated response like a gentleman
waiting for his lady to walk into a room before him
i mumble, "i'm enjoying you"
"i love you"
"i love you"
our raspy voices collide

but like all dreams
and like all baths
the warmth eventually
drains away

DIANA PHUONG, age 18

The Last Day of Our Lifetime Together

The last kiss is always the hardest,
lips barely moving together
but once they touch, it lasts no longer
than forgetfulness.
She was captivated by the architecture
of my elbow
firmly placed around her shoulder.
Then the darkness, lowering and lowering,
until our daytime visions
dissolved into dreams.
It was heavenly, but I had to do
what I had to do.
I handed her the letter.
A letter because I was strong enough
to start a relationship
but not man enough to break out.
She unlaced it,
fold flowing out of fold.
            She read it!!
In the time it took to sink in
she had a dozen questions.
I replied with an answer that gave
no answer.
Our eternal happiness now eternally gone,
darkness will be the point from which
we start.

L. C. HUGHLEY, age 17

Too Like Apollo

It was hailing

I just wanted
to feel wanted
him, solid over me
under me

his chest bare,
kissing my cheek
'goodnight, love'

I love how we touch
in semi-platonic comfort

I love how I misread
misinterpret a sort of longing
behind . . . this

He is too beautiful
too unlike Orpheus
and too like Apollo

to fall for me

PORTIA CARRYER, age 16

✳✳✳✳✳

the metaphors of space and time are nothing but a
memory now.
i have nothing to describe myself with,
i cannot put lines on paper that will encompass me.

and she lies beside me.
her eyes bore holes in my body so that
all i have left
are my eyes looking straight into hers.

and i float up, up
through the milky daylight and into the stars
where i am weightless and the novas explode around me.

there's nothing left for me but a blank canvas
and a paintbrush.
so what, now, should i paint?
should i paint the sorrows of love or the joys of
hatred?

maybe i should lie and contemplate what has happened
between me and the girl
that i would say i love.
or maybe, giving up hope of existing in peace,

i will put on a dress and spin into the lake,
float down, down in the peaceful swirling water
and land on the bottom and lie on the rocks for
the eternity of a kiss.

LILI MARTINEZ, age 14

Sonnet

I lied to you; I lied to them all,
I said it, and you willingly believed,
I said it again and I didn't fall,
I thought I'd won, I felt relieved.
The fallacy in my mind, you did toy with,
We met, and it began again,
I'd made myself something of a myth,
I was set off like a runaway train.
I could not stop, then I realized,
I've lost it; I'm no longer here.
I sat there pondering, paralyzed.
Metaphysics was my topic dear.
Who am I? Who are you?
Why the monkey, and not I, in the zoo?

SIMON JOHN WILLIAMS, age 15

To My Ex

Don't chew with your mouth open.
Don't tell me we're as close
as sand and water on the beach.
Now it's war: broken glass.
With gift after gift you set me up,
like ten pins in a game of bowling:
pin 1, a pager; pin 2, gold rings;
pin 3, a gold brooch for my mother;
pin 4, CDs for my brothers; pin 5, expensive
dolls, paying for all my hair styles
and money any time I wanted it.
Don't say you treated me like royalty.
I heard nothing but a cash register drawer.
Our relationship, loneliness,
a ringing phone with no answer.

STEPHANIE HARRIS, age 17

.directions south or north.

memoir, page one:
says something like,
when i was young, i etc
page two:
when i was older but still young enough to matter, etc
page three:
i gave my heart to a girl
the best i could and she
dropped it, etc
page four:
i gave my heart to a girl
and she ate it, etc
page five:
the only thing that mattered was the giving, see
and so on.
and someday i'll learn to stop writing poems for girls
no matter how much my eyes stray to the way
she holds a cigarette
and a baby with the same
tenderness, etc
no matter how much i like to touch her,
it won't warrant words on paper.

i'll write encyclopedias instead.

if i could pinpoint this
discomfort,
give it a name besides
vague,

i'd send it folded
in the middle of a hallmark card
to the end of the world
and drown it.

did i ever tell you
sometimes my face feels like a crossword puzzle
8-letter word for stupid
12-letter word for girl
the theme: what kind of question is that.
clues across and clues down,
a man scribbling with a
dying pen in the back
of a taxicab.

and sometimes i feel like the softest disaster
on scissoring legs.

maybe this is a letter.
to you, silly.
to you.

ELICHIA OWENS, age 18

Love Poem?

I can't write about love
'Cause I
Freak out about love
Never been touched
But I've touched so many lives with my love
I'm in disguise when I love
I'm in disgust when I hug
Unless it's
One of the blonde
Twins
I thought
I'd die
Just to fuck

Enough
It's torture
To me
Intercourse is horror
A borderline transformer
Whose passport is good 'til October

My verse
Is worthless
'Cause the birth
Of his first kid
Deserts him
So I purchase

A curtain
To strangle
My squirts in

What good are words
When your audience
Does not exist
Nobody sits
A minute
To stop and listen
To genius

My heart can't beat
'Cause gangrene
Is hanging
And tangled
In rigor mortis
While it holds on
To my arteries

My heart can't beat
Possibly
'Cause I've already stabbed me
Who the fuck said a love poem has to be happy

HALF, age 18

Love is Like

the sweetness of honey
falling from a bee hive.

You have to be careful
not to get stung.

HECTOR JASSO, age 16

girl/girl mouth/mouth

to get inside, beneath, between,
to repossess the fading scene,
to laugh with lips that stitch the seam,
to steal her strut, her breath, her dream,
to ball it up in sealing wax,
to let the hands dictate the facts,
to hide because the air is black,
to slip a nail into her back.

to grab for more of
sudden seeking
nipple peeking
coarse and dry,

to let each painted
inhale linger
lick your finger
wave goodbye.

LUKE M. RICKFORD, age 17

sarah & me

my perspective from this point is marred
dirty from the dried mud on the windshield
the stopped time inside
farmland blurred from speed
life turning over and folding back into itself
crazy laughter sucking into the wind
over the bumpy barren hills of eighty-four
decrepit crumbling carnegie
orange-spattered houston pumpkin festival
candy-colored sugar fumes poisoning us through canonsburg
I love our sacred rituals
the guilt of disenchanted catholicism mixed with
spontaneous revolution
the glory of teenage rebellion
drag racing with strange boys on 79 toward washington
kissing strange boys behind the haunted subway in bridgeville
sharing cherry cigarettes flying through south park,
gossiping about strange boys
dancing with strange boys at the dark splashed
neon rainbow sprinkles
rave in greentree
watching strange boys play bass and drums in glassport
sweat dripping, stomachs clenching
realizing they aren't as cute as we first thought
and running away before we can stop ourselves from flirting

ANNIE BOYD, age 17

✳✳✳✳✳

I am Poe's Lenore
Queenliest that died so young
Remembered in a requiem
A requiem from slandered tongue

Fitzgerald's Zelda
I was ever
Writing inspiration never
Looking back,
I was adored

Homer's Muse
That you may call me
Singing songs of twists and turns
Warning men
Of what they yearn

Many more times
In your learning
You will find me
Ever yearning
I am Poe's
Lost queen Lenore

Only this, and nothing more

BRONWEN CALLAHAN, age 14

Tall Glass of Beat

I hope you don't mind, but I
spent some lemonade on you this morning.
It took a couple drags to fall into the right state of mind,
borders are a bitch,
but your fucked-up tale of tantra helped
pass the time.

Your telltale scars were fading with
the spin my mind's given, just fading, out
of the picture.

(the only photo left of you is headless, anyway.)

funny how every single taste
my traveled mouth may greet carries some of
you, like stowaway molecules, though
I really don't oppose the thought
of you trapped under my tongue.

and this is the last time a
thought of your
piano-key teeth scraping the ears
within my skin will ever DARE
think of knocking. any lingering
notes have packed, and the
pedal is depressed.

MEHRON ABDOLLMOHAMMADI, age 15

The Perfect Guy

He gives me flowers,
Rings and notes,
Jewelry, makeup,
Other things.

I return the favors;
Anything for him.
I smile with joy —
No girl could ever be so lucky —

Until reality slaps me in the face.
It's fun to pretend,
But I must remember:
It's for her, not me.

VALERIE GARCIA, age 16

Jealousy

Across the room
You beckon men
With your fragrance.
Like bees to pollen,
They bumble by you.
I, too, fly closer,
Try to sip secrets
Of your charm.
I flit in shadows;
You bask in sun.
I sour, pucker;
My hopes rot
Like neglected fruit.

CATIE LYCURGUS, age 16

How I Tricked Myself into Losing Her

i'm not only talking about stolen stares
about late-night donut trips
and running up dark paved hills
panting   panting
with a girl i used to know
finding memories in shadowy leaves
and wishing night really obscured eyelashes
wishing night really was dark
our eyelashes never blended: hers black and mine covering
something forgotten
something forgotten like
curfew or bashful ignorance
something forgotten like her name against my gaze
like she would become

and i'm not only talking about how she never
talks to me directly anymore
only through stories about her sister and the dirty
sweatshirt that smelled like pee
but reminded her of him with its
unraveling hole above the left shoulder
so she wore it anyway
she wore it without a shirt underneath
and her bare brown skin shone through
like a little kid peeking through fabricated protection
i never mentioned the odor
or how i slowly was rubbed away—exhaled
as the garment became more constant in her life
than my heavy breathing next to her

i'm not only talking about etching my name
in the rotten bench outside the Ortega library
and coming back four years later
with a soggy pizza from Domino's
and a soaking hoodie covering curly matted hair
squinting to find my name
find some sort of affirmation that
i was alive and well four years ago:
sitting on the bench with braces
giggling behind lemon Popsicles
squinting
searching
only now i realize i can't even recognize
my own handwriting
the one thing i could claim
territory, carved approval, ownership
lost in the drifting rain

i'm not only talking about teaching myself how
to forget about the things i once convinced myself were essential:
red Windbreakers
mini Snickers bars
ticket stubs belonging to someone who walked too fast
falling asleep on the phone
finding wind tunnels
patches of sincere phrases

stripped stares stolen glances
all lost because
i don't know how to bring her back
how to find me inside her
how to make our eyelashes bleed again
to match the silence tacked between us.

DALIA RUBIANO YEDIDIA, age 15

Good Heart / Bad Intentions

I don't know what floats your boat but I'm sure I can rock it,
Commotion on relation ocean, my love potion is exotically hypnotic,
Gone off that notion I'm as hot for you as a vacation in the tropics,
I'm the Playboy Penthouse Hustler, game-wise I'm
chart topping in the top ten,
For the hototti hot salsa saucy mamacitas,
I'm Molotov in the palm and napalm talking,
With lava-hot saliva I'm beyond the strength of intoxicants,
Mister provocative to foxes, I'm that awesome,
Having bodies sweating in tops dropping bras and
launching panties at me because my prerogative
Is beyond the nonsense of misunderstandings,
I hold concentrations hostage whenever I'm romancing,
My target is to get a guarded goddess out of her garments
with the charm I harvest,
Yet alack and alas I harness my harshness,
To exalt the flyness of a highness to kiss her feet,
Try to recognize her shyness and lower my speed,
Oh woe is me, I grit my teeth and bear with
your wants and what you need,
Prince Charming armed with this sense of sensitivity
while lying underneath
Is a dormant volcanic inferno of a beast smoldering from the heat
Of controlling these hormonal emotions that roam within me,
I curse my dilemma to be a gentleman with freakish tendencies,
Festering like disease hidden in murky sceneries,
So the scenario to me is clear, that I'm the epitome
Of confliction, I want to understand you sweetie but

I'd rather rock you to sleep,

Cradle your dreams and cater to needs

All at the same time for thoroughbred is me,

Last of my dying breed going out trying,

To show with or without mine own survival how my love's undying,

So decide cutie cuz I need for you to choose

The view of my royal-purple hazes, shades and hues,

I know the truth is that you want a ruthless dude to seduce

And deduce your wants from your own trail of clues,

From the roots of your issue to your nail's cuticle,

You want to feel exclusively special and feel as if

you're the most beautiful,

Most high and so terrific that it's official that I'd be a fool for you,

And have sentimentality of value in my mentality

Of reality and fantasy like there is no equal and

I know that matter-of-factly,

As an Adonis I drift and travel in search of you, goddess,

The Don Juan pimping King of Hearts and Prince Charming,

So I'm sitting in this position with this confliction

Of mix as your best wet dream that when you daydream of,

you sweat, and mister right,

the sensitive type who provides you with feeling until you're

addicted off I,

But you fell in love with the whirlwind type,

I left your head spinning since I've entered in

the entrance of your life.

PRESTON JONES, age 17

Tristan and Iseult

As the wind breathes deep across the Cornish shores
and the fog clears away,
you can see their tree.

Still sturdy he stands, the hazel,
and wrapping her green silk fingertips across him
she clings, the honeysuckle.

One dying-since-the-day-they-were-born love,
one black-sail-white-sail confusion
realized-too-late fate,

one word,
black,
ended it all.

Through time and voice
we send the ship of the white sail out
and wait.

There a lesson grows,
a child learns;
an old woman knows,

Fate has left these two slain,
but what is left for those who remain?
Should we love or should we fear?
And if we choose fear, will their love die with us?

The hazel and the honeysuckle:
He with his bow and dark brow and
midnight eyes, sending messages
down the stream to where she waits.

With her hair like fire on a bed of white roses
in the darkness, betrayed, her heart waits
for rings and colored sails with signs,
the abandoning complete.

Years pass until the honeysuckle,
under a dark cloak, cries on the ship,
while the hazel lies in near-death,
eyes-closed-tight, sweating sleep.

He cries out, "Is it black?"
But for days no one answers,
and for days she is not but an instant away.
But the white sail is too late . . .

It is too late.

J. RIGGS, age 17

ramen noodles and hot chocolate

It's a dim red mars night and the yellow eyes of the car lot
gently wreck the image on the projector screen,
sitting near me, you draw me in with your quiet
interest and make me feel like
I could maybe move a little closer
and put an arm around your slim shoulders
That tonight, on a night of kids and moons and movies
you would love it, your warm skin pressed under my
short egg hair

We pass out our ramen noodles and hot chocolate,
to feed the masses of high school Galilee,
the odd combination of silver space-age chicken sauce
and Nestlé mix
As we return to our black and white aliens, I'm trying
to move a little closer, because I'm wondering
if I like you or just the idea of love tonight, and I realize
I don't know, but I could imagine us kissing and finding out
ramen noodles and hot chocolate
are a rarely paired delight and just
for a moment it would be different than the two night's
later wish of a sad poet-dreamer sitting with a cup of cold
hot chocolate, a half-eaten bowl of
noodles, and a stale hope

KYLE ENDERSON, age 14

(I'm Fuzzy)

Coat me, O my best beloved,
wrap me in your life's long sleeves —
a shirt you swore I wore before —
a rubber raft to float
about the bathtub.
How it kisses your crown
while eggshell tiles collide
like slow-mo explosions,
and I watch your eyes slip slowly —
like satin sheets upon a bed —
and wonder, am I nothing more
than sweet release?
    an aftertaste?
        an itch to scratch,
            then leave it be?
For none of those seem very real at all.
But now I'm small that's not the case,
I'm shrinking, so you squint to see; I'm fuzzy
and we're painted red and panting.

JOSHUA FU, age 17

The Truth of This Love

Take these shackles off my feet
So I can swim to the surface of your lies
Past your puppy-dog eyes
And countless denies
Of your true intentions

Release my heart from your hand
That keeps us in a bind
Our hearts and our lives intertwined
Like grapevines
And Brown Skin
And I can't tell where mine ends and yours begins

Take me from this darkness where I
Sleep and call your name
Wake and see your face
Pray for seven days' grace
And lick my lips and taste my past
Where yours were pressed to mine

Wish you'd stop pumping
Passion through my veins
With bats of your long lashes
That sting like twelve lashes

Wish there was a panacea for this pain
A little sunshine for this rain
That dampens my parade

So I can end this charade
Where I pretend like I don't love you
When I know
You know

I do

WILLIAM T. LANGFORD, age 16

trying to dance the story of you

barefoot
on the hardwood
   and the music is coming in soft
my hips are pressed against the bar
still, because the lights are off
you are standing just outside
with each breath I arch my back
and pull my elbows sharp, like wings
I can't tell through the distance how much you can see
   Because you are looking through the windowpane
   the way you could always look through me

the music grows and the lights spill onto the floor
the room gets hot
my arms bend through the air
trying to make a pattern from the pounding of sound
bending at the waist I am trying
to tell the story of you

I am spreading my movement across the floor
and still in your jacket you
   are just watching
   from the door
The way the mirrors toss my figure back and forth

I am trying to dance confusion
to feel the rhythm of the room
and my shoulders are trying to cut
through all the memories of you

I have surrendered to the music that
    suggests you in every count
I suspect that I will hear you
    somewhere inside of every sound
and now I'm counting on my reflection
to show me the pattern to where you are
I am relying on my intuition to dance the story of you so far
because, uncertain of the next step, I am frozen
and when I close my eyes I know
    my toes are pointed
    but yours are flexed

KIMBERLY SCHISLER, age 16

My Apologies

To all the males
Whose hearts have been
Impaled
By the spikes of my high heels
(Because it was on purpose
that I painted my toes Sonia's
Sexier Than Red
and slid the S form of my foot
through lacy black pumps,
that I happened to
lock
a pearl choker
onto my smooth neck,
and bound anklets round the thin of my leg
to add an innocent undertone of
bondage),
I was at fault for the
Silken blonde tresses
That fell upon my bare shoulders.
I enjoyed the confusion in your eyes
At my Monroe-meets-Hepburn dress
And if it were in me
I would have had
My way
With all of you
By now.
But it's not in me.
Like a van Gogh in a museum,
It's look but don't

Touch,
Even if you want to
Feel the texture.
Because,
Sirenesque,
I never keep the promise
My portrait seems to give.
Because I've cackled at your glances
Like a vicious bitch.
All this in hoping
That one of you
May not give me reason
To laugh,
To be amused,
That I might take advantage.
But until then,
Once again,
My apologies.

AMY COLLIER, age 15

Aside

Driving eastbound on the 17
I am just trying to make my way back home to you
You say you miss the way the leaves change,
Back in your Massachusetts
It's something about the way your face lights up,
As I take a drag off my cigarette.
It seems you and I are always working harder
Than any two people should have to
Just to find our cupboards empty
It's noon now,
And you're barely waking,
I wonder if you will even see the sun today

It's the production of everything you are trying to be
And the scene where you lose yourself
In my aside I have to say
That I have seen the way all of our faces have aged
Finding heaven in a bathroom stall,
I never thought any of us would die like this
It is more than obvious,
The ship is sinking,
But I was never one to be taken alive

Conversations so troubling
I wish I had the words to say,
To keep you from that door,
To keep you from walking away
You know that love is not forever
And I would be lying if I said I could change your mind
Yellow walls and white ceilings,
I can never sleep,
Thinking about you and your yellow walls and white ceilings

ZACHARY BOEHLER, age 18

✳✳✳✳✳

You're the bus driver on the Main Street line
Of the transit authority of my public mind.
I see you each day and pay you my fare,
But your inherent power makes me scared.

I sit on your bus with my headphones on
And think of you as I hear each song.
When I get off, I always say thank you,
But still it seems you don't have a clue.

What exactly do you think of me, sir?
I'd always had in my mind that you would concur.
I thought that I'd be able to win your heart.
Guess it's easier to speculate than to actually
take part.

MICHELLE, transgendered, age 15

Twelve

Young boys who fall in love,
they
want to love you
'til the sun burns out.

They live in the days
of knights and princesses,
gently taking your hand
and leading you
to the shining castle
that holds their young hearts,
give you every key to every door,
and
they'll gaze with intent
upon every precious
step   you   take,
and hold your head
against a warm chest
so you can mesh
with every beat.

Then they'll
run with you
out to the lawn
run their fingers
through your hair
brush your forehead
with soft lips
beneath the starry sky

while whispering
of sugar-coated tomorrows —
orange-sherbet sunsets,
purest white picket fences,
and crystal-clear oceans
with shells of undented texture.

But young boys who fall in love
one day
see that same sky
differently
now with
    broken innocence
pushing everything they've ever felt
into the shadows
of lost souls long forgotten

and then
they change all the locks.

CRYSTAL SALAS, age 14

Fat Kid

I am not fat.
Though I have been
scarred by
years of internal torment
that may warrant
the behavior I display,
making me slave to
sideways glances from
faces unknown,
empty compliments spoken in tones that
let me know that
somehow
I am desirable.
A stranger's touch can
become a crutch
used to
limp from bed to bed
to get some
drug-like fix of lust instead of
looking inside to
realize that
I may actually be worthy of love.
But
there's no need for
self-reflection
or recollection of
painful memories of how
I was teased for
being a little fat;

okay,
a lot.
But that's not the
point 'cause
now I'm the tease
so do what you please
just please,
please,
please,
make me feel
beautiful
or
wanted
so I can be haunted by that
chorus in my head
when I
jump into bed
with a
strange girl
or
strange man
reminding
me
that
I
am
not
fat.
I am not fat;
so long as I'm
all that to

someone,

anyone who

lusts after my body,

albeit

bruised and broken by

thoughts unspoken of a

fat little boy who

lives inside the

shell I am today,

crying out for

internal validation with

external gratification as

the only means to the end

when

I can pretend I'm

fulfilled.

This end won't justify the means

since

I have seen that

I am not fat

but I'm empty.

BEN CUEVAS, age 18

✳✳✳✳✳

You pretend that love is momentary,
And that you have sipped on the fire from the stars,
And danced and yelled with their glory in your veins,
Wrapped up like a diamond in a womb.
But you are only a snake in tall sunflowers
And I am but the love-struck maiden
Searching for blue skies.

FAAEZA KAZI, age 16

Testimony

I did it because red strawberries were falling from the sky.
The air was moist and the sky was clear.
A red fire was trying to get free.
There were no strangers there.
I did it because I wanted to try something new.
I wanted to fly above the trees.
Promises were made — to never leave each other,
but I would never do it again.
I did it because I was immature.
I did it because I wanted to be loved.

LaToya Jackson, age 17

You Had Your Chance

you had your chance
you had your turn
but you waited too long
and thats not my fault
now im gone tears run dry
are you crying for me
or are you crying for him

its you that makes me feel like im in a well
and its you that feeds me pills under my skin
and its you that ties me down when im up
and its you that shows me where I belong

you put me on trial
you said im blind
how could i have known
between right and wrong
now im here arms around you
willing to say you must go

PAUL STONE, age 16

Or Not

It was good.
then it wasn't
He was nice
then he wasn't
I was okay
then I wasn't
We both loved
then we didn't
It was always there
but it never happened

DISASTER, age 13

✳✳✳✳✳

In the presence of people
Packed in boxes,
Each wanting to be
Held

THOMAS ANDRADE, age 17

Denial

Reclining into a comfortable apathy
I
Watch you walk away
Tendons bouncing gleefully
In your retreating calves
(Good —
At least one of us is happy.)

Sing to myself how much you
Un-matter
To me

Floating in sentimental symmetry
I
See your departure
Clouds my vision
Trickles down each flushed cheek
(Believe me, Honey, those are tears of
Joy)

Smile.
Today love paints shades of grey.

LUKE M. RICKFORD, age 16

Indian Tea

It's noon
Where are you?
You promised me lunch
There's a café on the corner
With croissants and Indian tea
A gray pussycat hunts beneath the table
Searching for scraps of ham
And salami
She sneezes at the peppercorn
It's cute
We could've enjoyed that together
But I'll just lunch alone
And laugh at the little kitty by myself
I didn't want to share my croissant with you anyway

CHRISTINE S. STODDARD, age 15

✳✳✳✳✳

The stars, oh my god, the stars.
The curves of the earth
Falling away from the place you lie
Leaving an open sky
An open mind
A mind of thin clouds
That drift across the sea
A sea above you
It's power ready to engulf

Your wet back forgotten
You shiver
And don't know it
Who you're with
And not
Are forgotten

The stars
Nothing more
Nothing less
Just the stars

BEN JOHNSON, age 17

Sky in My Mouth

Kabuki beauty is cheap these days
I might be happy when I look in the mirror
If I liked the taste of watered-down coffee/Might.
But my mirror is a window
To the rain
Cool drops spattering through the screen
Singing on the wet streets.
I am beautiful to my bones
And I am happy
That I'm not holding your hand
Moist warm pockets of air
I never knew where the right chinks were
To slide my fingers through yours.
I wish you knew how to enjoy loneliness together.
I want to catch the raindrops in my mouth
Just wanna catch a little bit of sky in my mouth
My black hair like the night sky gushing down my back
Hips swaying in the breeze.

GRACE PETERSON, age 17

Hello, Love

Hello, my old "friend,"
Been a while since
You were here last.

I know why you've come,
And I'll ask you to leave me.

I know you're a delusion,
Conjured by a fickle one.
Who knows not what
She wants.

You light me up falsely,
Butterflies I haven't felt
Since a November years ago.

Warping me,
Like I'm drunk, lying
In those leaves again,
Asking for you,
Assured I really want you.

"Well," I'll say to you now,
"You've whirled me around enough,
I'll sit this one out,

too dizzy."

MICHAEL DOWELL, age 17

Detrimental to My Success

Yes, baby, I know you love me
but that is something I will not do
I will not choose to create the biggest snafu
Let me break it down for you like an inverse haiku:
I will not have sex with you
Sorry but it's true
'Cause my life, I do value
I do love you
Buuuuuuuuuuuuuut . . .
It's not happenin'
My legs stay shut like a tight clothespin
'Cause my Creative juices are flowing like my Zen
And if you stick your USB cord into my port
We might get a Micro
'Cause you wanted to embrace my tender torso
I'm sweet like a mango
But we can't tango
I have a code of conduct
That I refuse to let you destruct
Deduct from me
The energy I need
To be in all these APs?
I'm contemplating integrals, derivatives, where two points meet
Not our velocity or position when we get under the sheets
The right decision, I have to make it
If not, it'll follow me around later on in life;
I won't be able to shake it

Like let's say
A baby?
Maybe?
NO, 'cause God said no fornication
So I'll sit and wait patiently like I'm stuck in the train station
Until the day I walk down the aisle in my pretty white dress
I won't let sex
Be detrimental to my success

JAYLENE CLARK, age 17

Dreams of Ivy

Dreams of Ivy
At the corner café
under white moons
meticulous fingers rolling cheap tobacco
into rice paper
street performers
emerging from sidewalks
like chalk figures

"It's been too long," she whispers
over the rhythm of drums
floating through the air
arrows inching toward
her heart
beat
beat
beat
-ing the blood of ancestors
antiquated under her skin

dreams of infinite regress
which lie in brown eyes
and dreams of infinite progress
pouring out with each exhale
dreams
that hold the mysteries of luna

tics
tic
tock-ing time
on lunar nights with

Dreams of Ivy.

her fingers intertwined in mine
as smells of gyros streamline
from our breath
right below our eyes
to a man with little talent
but all the drive in the world
keeping him sitting
on that broken bucket
twang-twanging on his guitar
singing:
"Ey mambo, mambo ya"
in hopes that one of us will dance
Strip our clothes and dance!
because nudity brings humility and more money
for his bucket
dance

dance
dance
we dance.
"Ey mambo, mambo ya"
and he asks if we are lovers
"Sisters," I reply
her Vietnamese fingers
lining my African shoulders
both brown
both bold
both beautiful.

A-LAN HOLT, age 17

Mobius Heart

burns down his head,
rewinds his
rewind.

pretends he is stuck
in a stuck
loop.

bikes his bike to store
his store head,
heads to the store
to buy his
buy.

girls his
girl to repent his—
resent the girl
he's girled.

the world is all over
again, all
over.

PHILLIP TAYLOR-PARKER, age 17

What Is

The weary lilt of my hip against
the air, the presence of
blurry-faced strangers on
a shivering bus
is love.
Batting my eyes closed against
the crisp flapping of
clean laundry drooping over
yellow twine
is love.
A brightening ghostmoon against
dimming sky, my
room glazed with sunstrip light and
the slow static of the radio
is love.
Orange peels and
stiletto heels and
frothy meals with movie reels
is love.
I don't even know
what isn't.

JENNY XIE, age 15

Minus 64.5% of Us

A brain buzz without drugs
or lust, my girl is stupid
hips and holding hands
in cabs of trucks. Night.
Stars spark incarnations
in pupils upon asking, fizz
as a glass of soda.
Without limbs, girl and I
stand spinning, prowl
our own downtown,
bound by mutual gravity
in a swarm of thousands.
Shops bow to our monarch joints,
mark (with moist lips)
a trail of phantom warmth
as thick as dollar bills.

Girl and I just trip smoothly,
laugh, and mimic a moon
that is blind and pulsing.

PHILLIP TAYLOR-PARKER, age 17

Crave

I tell you
I glide with the wind,
I dive to the depths
Of every body of water,
I tower above the rest:
The weak, the tired,
The beaten and broken.
I stand strong,
Unafraid and young,
Slightly touched
With the beginnings
Of insanity.
Living and loving,
Enjoying the senses
I explore so brazenly
Each moment.
My eyes survey
The brassy descent
Of a glowing sphere.
The quivering, restless
Hum of voices,
Of melodies and harmonies,
Prick my ears,
Cooing gently,
Soothing the mind.
These precious experiences
Aren't enough.
They offer the relief
Of a teardrop

To a blazing wood.
I thirst for more:
To live through you,
To see with your eyes
What it means to be.
To feel the radiant
Heat of your body,
Melting the harshness
Of my solitary form.
Show me what I can be,
What love can mold
From two perpendicular lives.
Let me relish the chaos
Of creation.
I crave it.

CASSANDRA E. HUESER, age 17

Clinically Proven: Impossible

He can't gain weight.

I'll bet he has 3 nipples
nine toes
a bald spot
a vagina

That he kills stray cats
roasts them on the spit
in his bedroom

I'll bet his parents are
ex-rocker/biker dykes

That he grew up
not remembering how he got
the skull-shaped
scars — one on each
testicle

That his voice box
was jacked off
a dreamer

He's a Republican
Unreliable
a stand-up
a fraud

I'll bet his hair
is dyed

That his contacts are
. . . contacts

That his simplicity is so
complex — it flips

I'll bet he's vain
That he can't dance

That he's a tease
er — a fapper
A flirt

A curse
That he's a not-gonna-happen
I'm-too-cool kid

And an alcoholic

He'll beat me with
an ugly stick

A rapist

I'll spend my life

prosecuting his bad
habits—greasing wheels for
viruses, and selfish, dull
children

I'll consume myself—
Imploding into a
panting dog

Lustful
abominable
smirking

Infinite hair follicles
two nipples
the proper appendage
20/20 vision

Unable to gain weight.
He'll still be
one of a kind.

NADIA KENT, age 16

Terminal

I
wait for
the A train
her

Stink muggy smog at 10 p.m.
Alone in the concrete cave
Alone in a hole
Alone without her
Mile-wide massive walls
Grandeur
But it feels so confining
Around my chest

Stare down the black-hole tunnel
Of course, no light comes
Bleary impatience
She must be impatient
Hot dust streaks by
My eyes burn
Everything burns
Feel tired
Sit down
Graffiti-rainbowed bench
Need a smoke
Hard to breathe in recycled air
Pull off jacket
Just need a little nap
Wait for the echo to stop

Going to make up
Need to say sorry
I wasn't thinking
I love you
I just need to slow down
We need to slow down
Everything's slowed down
We're going to grow old together

My chest burns with thirst
The gaping-throat tunnel smiles
And swallows me

She waits for
me

JOSEPH, age 17

Ode to You in Beat

So here it is
Graphed planted sprouting to the surface for your information
A series of words that make sense
Perfect
Remembering the moment you're in kind of jazz
Feeling as a way of commutation
Being beautiful methodically, mad crazy quiet clean stuff
Feeling invincible in your untouchable rinse-cycle vulnerability
And loving the cruelty of it all
That's what I live for
Crisscrossing the median strip of conformity in half jumps
without shoes Knowing imagination can take that craving
away and turn it into sugar
Hearing Kerouac turn into kerosene with a few jumbled lines
about the youth Feeding me adjectives like I've never tasted before
Getting all my vitamins from Ginsberg and Fuck America and
Your Atom Bomb type of shit that leave messages on my
machine about Liberty and Freedom and all those other Words
we can't look up in our white Christian dictionary without the
proper credentials
Because me loving you is a sin
But when I loved the hard-hitting boy down the street who
left his name in bruises on my arm and the half-man who
tore himself from me after I had nothing left to give
That was love That was right
And you are my one-way ticket
To a world without punctuation
Poets have so many rules that define their yearning for a boxless

society Maybe beat was just another citation in the rule book
Like see-section-five-paragraph-six kind of mess
Step on the pedal, generation, and get this shit going
Because regardless of what he might say, I know he inhaled
And all power to him
Because I inhale the scent of you without apologizing
And I think the world would be a better place without
clothes or legislators or those twenty miles that
separate our bedrooms
I wish I could ingest some change now and then for the
world that's getting closer and closer to ending its own
broken-down busted muffler-on-the-fritz life Bustling down
my street making so much noise it's waking up the little
boys and making them grab their guns and it's waking up
the little girls who just got done tying their ribbons
But it's not loud enough to wake the good-for-nothing coals
we keep throwing in the fire so nothing gets done
I keep hitting that damn radiator
And it won't turn on the masses
So I'm in the process
Buried deep in the process
Up to my arteries in the process of cleansing myself
Because if beat were a woman, I'd make passionate love to her
And she'd make crazy untamed glass-shattered love back
And it would be beautiful and untainted and none of those
adjectives Fred is so fond of using
Rhyme would suffocate reason in my womb so all that's birthed
to me is insanity
Because it's insane that I can't give what you want without
breaking a law Loving you ain't a crime it's an excuse for being
So stop pointing dirty fingers at me

Try to shame me, counterculture
That's all your mess is good for
And I can't see it working anytime soon
Not while I've still got fingers to write with
And a girl that loves me more than I deserve

EMMA ZELDIN, age 17

The Chronicles of Love

Love is when the heart ruptures into an abyss
of indefinite definitions of perplex emotion.
Caricatures of one's self sharpen like a pencil
that sketches the fates of many.

Love is as inescapable as God's calling
to his vast heavens,
as unexpected as tomorrow
forever claims to be.

Is there a universal raffle?
Perhaps names are shaken in the Dipper amongst the stars;
all the things that one would denounce in others are forgiven
with a soft forbearance candidly expressed through the heart.

The chronicles of love are immense in this world
of "I love you's" and false pretenses,
wrapped in threads of mind and mixed emotion,
blanketed by the unknown eyes of the mysterious.

ANTHONY HILL, age 17

Ode to Her Skin

I want to walk out into the night
And cross the two streets
Between us.
I'll sneak into your room
And turn on every electric light.

Light will be everywhere, filling the corners —
From the ceiling, from your desk, up from the floor,
Beside your bed, out of the fishbowl,
Light, light, light, light dribbling down the walls and
Puddling into the folds of your warm blanket.

Then,
When I can look at you from every bright angle,
I'll find you a new name,
Something that fits close to the skin;
Smooth, sleek, low-cut
Something, anything but
"Beautiful" —

Tired, bruised-up "Beautiful" —
Which has been dragged through the mud
By a thousand buffaloes in love.

LUKE M. RICKFORD, age 17

a pause for poetry.

kissing your face, your neck, your shoulders
tastes like home
made ice cream fresh from the freezer
lingering on my lips, lips
pushing, pulling, puncturing language
into dartboards across continents and
you have been with me wading in
waters and wandering
toward north stars
toward freedom over
atlantic migrating patterns where
ducks move like boomerangs, arrows
pointing south is home or
temporary residence where
we are illegal residents swimming
across riverbanks and
wallowing in wet mud like
children, happy to be dirty because
purity comes complimentary and
dirt shows net worth like
zen like peaches in spring and
when winter comes we are silence in
a world surviving off subconscious
obsessions and screams and temper
tantrums from two-year-olds and I am
kissing your face, your neck, your shoulders
and you taste like home.

A-LAN HOLT, age 17

Untitled

When morning eased over us in flames, we walked along the beach
where the palms bowed low and the ocean kissed our feet.

In the new sun's glow, your dark hair caught
and became precious in its aftermath.

I remember that even the birds stopped singing.

A dusty quiet reigned. But not for long.
Waves came.

And in the new sun's glow, your dark hair caught,
precious, but somehow rarer in the aftermath.

J MIDGLEY, age 16

a note from a late romantic

meet me at the coffeehouse
after the concert.

the orchestra can play
that *adagietto* movement for us

and as the harpist plucks
chords
we'll be gently tumbling
into crevices
of curls and cadences
landing on lips.

so come from behind your bass
and open your stringed arms
for this bow will stroke
your fears and caress
your sorrow
until we are freed
of our wooden frames.

then everyone will know
our symphony.

BONNIE KAVOUSSI, age 17

Song

The rhapsody of heart and soul
Telling stories
   Long untold
      Of love and lust
         Of death and life
         But can it be
         Of you

         And me?

COLE LUTKE, age 14

Tonight

We are shades of gray:
Our gay laughter too bright
for this end, for this night.
These are the rules we have bent:
Gravity
Geography
Acoustic versus electric
Size eight
The First Flush

I have never had to wait for you
always next to me
We will stretch our arms
across the nation and be
Magic as we can.

Tonight, we are in black and white
Our bodies an amalgam of extremes
and we will cry, and say it's the smoke
and hope the end won't come,
Not tonight.

PORTIA CARRYER, age 16

Memories of You

I miss you less than I thought I would.
I miss you more than I think I do.
I want you less than I thought I did.
And I love you more than I ever knew.

MARY KATHERINE MEADOWS, age 16

Raindrop Songs

This sounds like raindrop songs,
Me knocking on your back door
As you read coffee-cup obituaries
And we both find ourselves receding with
paper-cut assumptions.
When the stars fall
You proceed to follow,
For lately we look less like the American dream
And more like an American tragedy.
We struggle to understand the sirens in a silent film,
When the subtitles are in a language that we do not speak.
Confusion in responsibility,
I will just stick to jazz.
Yes, jazz, and the way you lift your eyes up to greet mine
As you answer the door.

ZACHARY BOEHLER, age 17

Credits and Acknowledgments

"Love Song" by Deneshea Richey was previously published in *Zero Gravity*, InsideOut Literary Project, 2006.

"Bodies Can Move This Way" by Gia Harris was originally published in *Umläut*, Summer 2006, Vol. 3, San Francisco School of the Arts.

"Detrimental to My Success" by Jaylene Clark was previously published in different forms online at www.harlemlive.org/arts-culture/poetry/poetryslamwinner/detrimentalsuccess.html, 2005; www.youthradio.org/poetry/index.shtml, March 2007; and www.mxwlmagazine.com/JayeneClarkDetrimental.html, March 2007.

"Sitting on the porch swing . . ." by Joseph Lindblad was previously published online as "Suburbia" at The Slam, Carus Publishing, www.cricket-mag.com/theslam.htm, 2005.

At a Candlewick Press dinner, Patricia Strawn, an extraordinary high school librarian from Houston, told me that the most requested subject in her library, by far, was love poems. She said boys liked to copy them to give to girls, and girls loved to read them. She suggested that I compile an anthology to meet the demand.

The idea could never have become a book without the help of my friends, old and new. Robert Jaffe and Traci Gourdine alerted their Innerspark students, whose poetry was consistently outside the box. Through Terry Blackhawk, Robert Fanning, and Echo McMahon, I was able to access the compelling poetry from InsideOut Literary Arts Project in Detroit. Robert Fanning and Bob Bowles went way out of their way to find authors.

Heather Delabre, former slam-master of Carus Publishing's *Slammables*, assisted me in contacting excellent poets from her website. The editor of *I Am Not a Juvenile Delinquent*, Sharon Charde, spent hours gathering permissions from her hard-hitting poets. Jamie Hanmer, Kristen Lo, and Paul Dunlap spread the word, as did Eden Beck, Sherry Stephenson, Cal Vande Hoef, Lynn Evarts, and many other teachers and librarians. I received many submissions from all over the world because of Sharon Levin, patron of children's literature, who spread the word through her Listservs.

Students Sharon Cooper, Katie Chow, Ellie Moore, and Nicolette Bocalan kindly encouraged writers to submit their work. Gia Harris and Heather Woodward from San Francisco School of the Arts, Mahru Elahi of WritersCorps, and Lily Walters of Allpoetry were vital to the book.

I'm indebted to Lee Bennett Hopkins, who supported me wholeheartedly in my efforts to ensure diversity in the collection. A big thank-you goes to my sons Tom and Dave Franco for giving me thoughtful, insightful feedback on the nearly finished collection, and to Maria Damon for her constant encouragement.

I sincerely appreciate the work of all the poets who submitted to the anthology, whether or not your poetry made it into the book.

Thank you to everyone who helped me without my knowing, and to anyone I have inadvertently left out of these acknowledgments.

Finally, I am deeply grateful to my wise editor, Mary Lee Donovan, who understood what I was up to and who values the poets in this anthology as much as I do.